SOS

MISSING

Tales Of The Lost

Edited By Donna Samworth

First published in Great Britain in 2020 by:

Young Writers
Remus House
Coltsfoot Drive
Peterborough
PE2 9BF
Telephone: 01733 890066
Website: www.youngwriters.co.uk

Printed and bound in the UK by BookPrintingUK
Website: www.bookprintinguk.com
YB0451W

FOREWORD

IF YOU'VE BEEN SEARCHING FOR EPIC ADVENTURES, TALES OF SUSPENSE AND IMAGINATIVE WRITING THEN SEARCH NO MORE! YOU'VE FOUND WHAT YOU'VE BEEN LOOKING FOR WITH THIS ANTHOLOGY OF MINI SAGAS.

We challenged secondary school students to craft a story in just 100 words. In this second installment of our SOS Sagas, their mission was to write on the theme of 'Missing'. They were encouraged to think beyond their first instincts and explore deeper into the theme. The result is a variety of styles and genres and, as well as some classic lost and found tales, inside these pages you may find characters looking for meaning, memories erased or even whole populations disappearing overnight.

Here at Young Writers it's our aim to inspire the next generation and instill in them a love of creative writing, and what better way than to see their work in print? The imagination and skill within these pages are proof that we might just be achieving that aim! Well done to each of these fantastic authors.

CONTENTS

Niamh Katie Roberts (11)	63
Emily Jane Davitt (12)	64
Jack Burrill (12)	65
Mia Hanmore (12)	66
Joseph Money (14)	67
Harry Neath (14)	68
Brandon Butterfield (11)	69
Elsie Turner (11)	70
Eva Tregonning (12)	71
Nevaeh Bailey (11)	72
Alfie Lee (14)	73
Noah Jebson (13)	74
Niamh Morton	75
Zachary Shaw (12)	76
James Morris-Iliffe (12)	77
Maddison Alice Caunce (13)	78
Olivia Wilde (12)	79
Lucy Montgomery	80
Grace Burgess (12)	81
Katie Workman	82
Alessio Ruocco (12)	83
Dylan William Nicholas (13)	84
Maddox Bellew (12)	85
Alfie Arden-Turner (12)	86
Joseph Ball (11)	87
Kayleigh Barnes	88
Madison Evans (11)	89
Abbie Williamson (11)	90
Tom Healey (11)	91
Harry Butcher (14)	92
Skye Philburn (12)	93
Imogen Lyne (15)	94
Isabella Hill	95
Arron North (14)	96
Ben Hoyle (13)	97
Amelia Ashworth (12)	98
Amelia Palmer (12)	99
Charlotte Gittins (15)	100
Lauren House (13)	101
Jessica Ramsden (12)	102
Lucas Wilmot (11)	103
Katerin Hiffe (12)	104
Archie Walsh (11)	105

Lauren Murray (12)	106
Mary-Anne O'toole (12)	107
Ella Chalk-Derby (12)	108
Cohen Ballentine (12)	109

Montrose Academy, Montrose

John Dutch (16)	110
Roan Angus (13)	111
Paige Buchan (17)	112

Olchfa Comprehensive School, Sketty

Hannah Cameron (13)	113
Heidi Rodenburg (12)	114

Parkhall Integrated College, Antrim

Jadyn Coates (12)	115
Saffron Woods (12)	116
Jack Daley-Beck (14)	117
Ryan Empey (13)	118
Eva Hamitlon (13)	119
Sophia Dundee	120

St John Baptist CIW High School, Aberdare

Olivia Heath (12)	121
Madeleine Mold (14)	122
Amy Smith (11)	123
Bailey Smith (12)	124
Keira Taylor (12)	125
Jack Salmon (12)	126
Ruby Jones (12)	127
William Thomas (12)	128
Isabella Towers (12)	129
Ciaran Chiggey (11)	130
Theo Christopher (12)	131

St John's Academy, Perth

Pia Aylas Burghard (12)	132
Rholmark Colanse (12)	133
Olivia McNaughton (12)	134
Marcus John MacNeill (12)	135
Hanna Długołęcka (13)	136
Olivia Elder (13)	137
Georgie Balla (12)	138

St Richard's Catholic College, Bexhill-On-Sea

Chloe Smith (12)	139
Nico Luscombe (12)	140
Jeseena Joseph (13)	141
Oliver Ardley (12)	142
Alex Hards (13)	143

Thomas Telford School, Telford

Phoebe Hands	144
Lily Dodds (12)	145
Freya Preece (12)	146
Milly April Slater (13)	147

THE STORIES

The Fall

The girl froze. Her long, silky hair crossed her cold, pale face; her pupils retracted. She couldn't take them off the giant beast before her. Then the adrenalin kicked in, her entire body swerved as she began sprinting away from the foul creature. She could hear the pounding footprints following her as she hurdled jagged rocks and stray roots. Suddenly, her foot became stuck on a large grabbing root half-submerged and it propelled her into a very deep, dark hole. The beast turned and ran while the girl screamed as she fell down into the black nothingness below.

Rhiannon Hill (12)
Hastings High School, Burbage

Missing Point

Walking through the crowded school, with one hand carrying your bag, the other in your pocket. Moving through these hallways of judgement, people stare with various emotions - though none of them positive. Smaller kids intimidated, popular kids disgusted, teachers disappointed. They think you're the 'bad one', always in trouble, never doing work. But they're missing the bigger picture, they can't see you helping out at the animal shelter or working at the weekend to eat. They don't know you walk miles every day as you can't afford the bus. That's why you're always late. They're all just missing the point!

Jake Ansell (15)
Hautlieu School, St Saviour

Dear Father

I try to get up but floods of memories come back to me of us. Times weren't that great, were they? You weren't a good father. I'd wait outside in the rain, waiting for someone to save me from your absence. At home you'd lie intoxicated as ever. I watched you drown yourself, your life washing away. We don't talk anymore, we never really did. Now your presence is gone, I'm free. You're just a missing part of my life. I'm strong enough and learnt from the pain. So I'll get up now the rain has gone. From, your son.

Rhys Jones (17)
Hautlieu School, St Saviour

Ring, Ding, Ping

An echo in my head, bouncing from wall to wall, ceiling to floor, flowing in circles as if riding on the highways of my skull. I breathe it, I eat it, I sleep it, I need it! It pings, it rings, it dings, each wave an unsettling and yet comforting symphony barring thoughts from a foreign mind. But now it's gone. Without it mountains could fly and planes could fall and I would be here, sipping my Coke, on my couch, completely unaware. For hours I have looked, looked everywhere. It's gone. Missing. But in the silence, there's peace.

Henrique Pires (15)
Hautlieu School, St Saviour

Missing Myself

What do you miss? Your childhood friends? Your old dog? I miss myself. I miss being free in my mind. Being able to make my own way. I miss my old life. Seasons change, and with them we change. The harsh cold of winter closes us in, whilst the warmth of summer exhilarates and revives. I miss the days that I stood my ground. That I didn't change. Where playful whispers were just whispers and where sundown meant sweet dreams. I miss when the shackles of my thoughts didn't tie me down or hold me back. I miss being me.

Mitchell Rennie (15)
Hautlieu School, St Saviour

The Trip

My hands. They were gone. I was drifting in and out of sleep but I couldn't, I had to find them. I had to find my hands. The water in my room was rising at an alarming rate and there were fish in the water. I had to do something and fast. I had submerged myself and had one last look for my hands. Useless. There was only one option: I kicked through the double glazed window and threw myself off the third storey. I had my hands back but my legs were broken. I was never taking drugs again!

Joe Bougeard (16)
Hautlieu School, St Saviour

Ten Weeks

It's all still so familiar. The smell of her perfume lingers at the tip of my nose as if she were here ten minutes ago. But no, not ten minutes, it's been ten weeks and three days since my wife went missing, working two jobs to cover her half of expenses. Anything that comes up linked to her restores my hope. Suddenly, there's a knock at the door, there's a letter on the floor. I open it and inside there is a sum for her ransom...

Keisha Huby (14)
Hautlieu School, St Saviour

The Other 99.1 Percent

The sun stared down, directly onto me and sympathetically allowed a bit of the outdoors to creep into my room like times before, leaving everlasting scars. The rays of light blazed through the curtains and bounced off the green walls, crawling inwards, crushing any hope left whilst burning my susceptible skin. A draught slithered through the untouched window, brushing past my delicate body. The curtains revealed a new universe rarely witnessed. All I was missing was within touching distance. However, ever since my allergies were discovered, I knew I was never the other 99.1 percent... At least I could imagine.

Katie Healey (13)
Hodgson Academy, Poulton-Le-Fylde

Missing

Running, the forest had no end. As I bolted past the soggy, lifeless leaves they seemed to gain consciousness and slice my pale cheeks. I was as cold and as lonely as the dead. Suddenly I sped into something - a wall-like structure yet not visible! Punching, kicking, screaming, panicking - I couldn't get any further than the seemingly non-existent barrier. Instantaneously, a screen appeared. It was my mother frantically looking for something. Crying uncontrollably. A voice bellowed from above, "I've sent a note of ransom. Until they pay up you will be declared missing, presumed dead..."

Aaliyah Michelle Jobey (15)
Hodgson Academy, Poulton-Le-Fylde

Reality

Why couldn't I remember? As I got thrown on the ground I heard unidentifiable mumbles towering over me like I was an unwanted nuisance. Scraped across the stony, frigid floor, they eventually unmasked me with alacrity. Finally being given back my missing, needed sense, I scanned my surroundings to see the obliterated city. My implacable mind focused on the derelict, apocalyptic buildings. Reality soon changed and flashed before my lifeless eyes; the rose-tinted glasses I wore covered up the truth and showed the once perfect past, society lived. What happened here? Why are people missing from reality?

Sophie Beatwell (14)
Hodgson Academy, Poulton-Le-Fylde

The Lost Girl

They will never find me. I'm Alex and I'm fourteen. You probably don't understand what I first said so let me explain... When I was thirteen I had a best friend called Lyssy. She was so kind. One night, Lyssy called me and I answered. "Hi Alex," she said, suspiciously.
I replied, "Hey, what's up?" She never called on Friday as she had tennis.
She said, "Come to my house?"
I was confused but I said, "Okay."
I arrived at her house and she pulled me in and I fell into the basement...
I'm trapped by my so-called friend! Help!

Chantelle Jay (12)
Hodgson Academy, Poulton-Le-Fylde

The Missing

It felt like a year ago since she went missing...
We sat in the police station, waiting for an officer. My parents were silent. My sister was gone. Where? Nobody knew, or did they? Mum nervously turned to Dad and looked him dead in the eyes. "Where is our baby?" Mum whispered. Dad didn't respond. Instead, he walked to an officer and asked him in despair, "Where is she? Where is my child?" The officer quietly replied, "We don't know, Sir. I apologise." Dad sat back down again. Little did they know, I was the cause of her going missing...

April Southern (12)
Hodgson Academy, Poulton-Le-Fylde

Missing

Jamie Dodge was next in line - worried, nervous, scared, mixed emotions filled my rose-red insides. Picked up, launched; as I tumbled through the air I saw a coffee-coloured pond. Elegantly, moisturised, hand-like material. Picked up by the head and dunked into this steaming liquid, my bottom half turned soggy... part of me was missing. A large scream echoed around the room, like a lion's prey this beast screamed with great pain. Red goo poured from my insides, the pond erupted and spewed everywhere. Although it was coffee I, Jamie Dodge, all this time had been a Jammie Dodger.

Oscar Postles (12)

Hodgson Academy, Poulton-Le-Fylde

Gone Under

Missing, presumed dead. 5pm, 3rd August - Bondi Beach
Sally Webster went under. Frightened, worried, anxious:
lifeguard Mouse paddled out to his patient. Like he was
magic, everything turned into slow motion as he watched
Sally drown right before his eyes. He paddled as fast as he
could but when he got to the spot she was last seen,
nobody was there. Devastated, he paddled back.
Helicopters were sent out to look for Sally.
Hours after the last sighting, a boy ran up to the lifeguards
saying, "My mummy went for a swim three hours ago; I've
not seen her since..."

Kristen Beswick (12)
Hodgson Academy, Poulton-Le-Fylde

Forever Alone

First it was my English teacher, then my grandma, now my dog. Ever since the 25th of December, my life has become isolated and secluded. Tomorrow, tonight, ten minutes... I could be seized too. Anxiously I pace through the tranquil, desolated streets in hope to find others. Where is everyone? No one is here. People just vanished into thin air, leaving no trace. My mind every day loses belief; will I forever be abandoned and miserable? Sluggishly, my mind's crumbling and perishing away. Disappointed, my soul shall continue to rot like a dead corpse. Am I not the one missing?

Natalie Welch (13)
Hodgson Academy, Poulton-Le-Fylde

I Don't Need Him

I'm hated, hindered and heavily abhorred. Routinely, strangers will nonchalantly put out their cigarettes on my shirt. My family are sheep who have disowned me, they hate me. At my current home I've had death threats sent to me like leaflets for a local butchers. Multiple times I have been beaten up or attacked like Joseph Stanislav who was attacked in February 2020 or the two high school students who were attacked in March 2020. Why? It's because we're gay; they say we're 'missing God'. Maybe we are but we don't need God, we have each other.

Lily Williams (13)
Hodgson Academy, Poulton-Le-Fylde

Missing

'Missing, presumed dead...' The news flashed across the screen. A week ago a boy went missing. Playing, climbing, exploring: all the child was doing when he vanished. Policemen surrounded the house as his parents were taken away but it wasn't their fault. It was simply chance. He had been at the wrong place at the wrong time. That's all. Yet the police still thought someone had kidnapped him. But they were looking in all the wrong places. They needed to turn their gaze away from the ground and into the heavens, for the thing that took me wasn't human...

James Fallon (12)
Hodgson Academy, Poulton-Le-Fylde

Missing

May 14th, the day of my escape.
After the last guard checked the prison hallway, it was time.
I unlocked the vent with a crowbar I had moulded the
previous night, then flushed the evidence. I crawled through
the claustrophobic ventilation system and peeked through
the vent. I observed the officer doing his night-time patrol.
Swiftly, I climbed out and tentatively made my way to the
bike repair shed. Suddenly, I was lit up by a flashlight,
followed by a shout. I collected the glider I made, jumped off
the building and flew over the electrical fence. I was missing.

Daniel Thomson (12)
Hodgson Academy, Poulton-Le-Fylde

Who? Where? When? What?

Why couldn't I remember? Any of it! Empty, empty like a dark hole. A pin drop could have been heard - I could feel my unsettling nerves beneath my skin. My bones rattled. The coward side of me really was showing through! Where were they? What happened? They should be here! No answer, nothing! The wind howled, the trees danced and the leaves shivered. Right now I felt like a useless leaf. I quickly wanted to change my dampening mood. I still couldn't get over why this had happened. I couldn't just sit here though. I needed to do something... *Bang!*

Ava Weston (12)
Hodgson Academy, Poulton-Le-Fylde

Missing

Part of me was missing; half of me felt lost. He was gone. The day I lost my heart. My husband was missing. I couldn't see myself but the sensation of my burning cheeks envisioned that the Niagara Falls was my tears. I felt empty like no one was there. I could feel the warmth of their hands on my quaking shoulders as thoughts raced through my head, *what happened to him?* Crushing, heartbroken, lost. There was nowhere to turn apart from the policeman handing me an envelope. The ransom night arrived. Its bold words read: 'Missing, presumed dead...'

Lucie Emery (15)
Hodgson Academy, Poulton-Le-Fylde

They'll Never Find Me

They'd never find me here... The police sirens are screaming out. I was on the loose...

"A 24-year-old man is on the run, just escaped from New York Metropolitan Police Stations. Please report him if you see him. The FBI are offering a £50,000 reward for reporting his location."

The news was all about me escaping I had to hide quickly. The police were looking for me everywhere, they were all around the streets and the highways were being stopped and searched. I had a car but I wouldn't be able to leave the state. I was done for...

Ben Rollins
Hodgson Academy, Poulton-Le-Fylde

Aliens

"No, wait, stop! Argh..." James woke up with a startle. He looked around his room, looking for evidence that might suggest his dream was real. As he lay back down his radio started making a bizarre sound. He stared at it with a puzzled expression.

The next day, James set off for school. Something wasn't right, everyone seemed... sad! As James walked into school he tried to give his best friends a high-five. They just stared at him. James was about to walk off when he noticed something coming towards him. It wasn't human... "Argh!"

Lucy Huggard (12)
Hodgson Academy, Poulton-Le-Fylde

Year 3000 - Life In A Dystopian Future

Year 3000. The world is a nightmare. There is no life, trees, light or hope. Day by day, we wake up to this same neglected, deadly atmosphere. Tranquillity lingered until a thundering bang. Everything was a blur. I couldn't see anyone or anything; not even my family. Feeling so alone, my heart broke and in no time shattered into pieces as tears trickled down my face. The world that I'd called a nightmare was now a devastating tragedy. Our worst-case scenario had finally become a reality. The human race had become extinct, apart from me. I never knew why.

Grace Amu (13)
Hodgson Academy, Poulton-Le-Fylde

Missing

As I tiredly stumbled down the flooded path, a TV gleamed through a window showing a couple crying tears, crocodile tears. The woman whimpered, "Oh, I just wish I had my boy back."
I mockingly laughed as I continued down the path. "That isn't really them, they're pretending!" I said. Suddenly a copper approached me. I put my hood up as he explained he was looking for a boy who matched my description. I was the description. I said no and the copper walked off as an evil smirk ran across my face and I sprinted off into the night.

Reece Clark (13)
Hodgson Academy, Poulton-Le-Fylde

Derelict Memories

Hot, sweating, dehydrated. I woke up to a blurred range of greens. The blistering heat that throbbed like fire stung to breathe in. Although one deep breath obliterated my vulnerable nose, it discovered a flow of harsh odours. As though I hadn't eaten in months, I sank my teeth into bitterly sour fruit, leaving a tingly aftertaste. Questions put me into a rattle... why couldn't I hear? It was like part of me was missing. The throbbing silence was almost deafening. The jungle screeched and bawled, yet I only heard rumbling hums from derelict memories...

Summer Holroyd (14)
Hodgson Academy, Poulton-Le-Fylde

Gone

The place was empty - this surreal place where children smiled every day with no worries. Memories of my parents bringing me here flooded my mind and I felt my body begin to turn numb. Miniature, enclosed areas where they used to stand surrounded me, sending paranoid shivers down my spine. I never thought it would come down to this. I pictured a younger version of myself beaming at them, attempting to gain their attention yet they were usually too busy taking in the sun or being fed to acknowledge me. I became light-headed. At this point humans became extinct.

Rebecca Guillot (14)
Hodgson Academy, Poulton-Le-Fylde

The Heart's Missing Light

Darkness, everything was lost. No love, no hope, no nothing. Life's chance at ever returning was now and forever missing. Ten years had passed since that fateful day and ever since, the bond had grown weaker and more disposable. Always thinking he would never move on and hoping that this day wouldn't come. The only positive outcome of this loss was the release of the constant wondering: *when would I go missing from my place? As I will always be missing from that wishing place. The place that loved ones go. For I am the star that went missing.*

Jessica Paley (13)
Hodgson Academy, Poulton-Le-Fylde

The Empty Grave

The place was empty, Mona's grave was empty! I couldn't believe this, who would dig up Mona's grave? You could see hand marks in the mud. Who? What? When? Why? My heart skipped a beat... "Was she buried alive?" I asked myself. No, that couldn't have happened. I heard footsteps in the distance. There was a gunshot. My heart pounded in fear. *Do I scream or do I remain silent?* I thought to myself in horror. "Was that Mona's killer? My life was threatened. All I can remember from then is darkness and my head hurting...

Olivia Jackson (11)
Hodgson Academy, Poulton-Le-Fylde

Survivior

From that day forward, a part of me has been absent. No more smiles or jokes or shared laughter. Just silent pain. The undesirable images are still vivid in my mind... Blood trickling from my pale fingertips, bullets eternally etched into the walls and the torment of my sanity being ripped away from me. It was cold, empty and absent from sound; the emotionless horizon emitted a dull light illuminating the heinous scene before me. Bodies lay dispersed around the murder site. The memory provoked my cheeks to become wet. I thought surviving was a blessing...

Rosemary Leadbetter (15)
Hodgson Academy, Poulton-Le-Fylde

Missing, Presumed Dead...

Missing, presumed dead. They'll never know what really happened. Never know the truth. I couldn't find anything and I started to panic. As I sprinted the trees started to become scarcer and a building emerged. It didn't seem right but the horrendous circumstances disagreed with my gut! When I entered, the smell of damp wood and rotting meat was overpowering. As I walked on I realised the floor was red. Stained. Pools of blood covered everything and my heart stopped. Footsteps grew louder. I ran but the door wouldn't open. I was trapped...

Paris-Anne Patrick (14)
Hodgson Academy, Poulton-Le-Fylde

Part Of Me Was Missing

Part of me was missing... but what was it? Lazily, I rolled out of bed and stared at my reflection in the mirror, looking at my body closely. No body parts were missing. No teeth! Nothing! Confused and distressed, I strolled around my house, checking every object in sight. Suddenly, there was a strange pain in my heart. I ignored it and got on with my day as normal.

Late, anxious, panicky, I sprinted down the road. Everything went black. Where was I? An angel-like figure came towards me. Instantly my heart felt full. I knew what was missing... Mum?

Loti Bailey (14)
Hodgson Academy, Poulton-Le-Fylde

Missing Girl

Midnight struck on the small black clock when the door rang. Nobody was prepared for the trauma that greeted my half-asleep mum as she opened the door to a beaten and bruised teenage girl. She didn't know us and we thought we didn't know her until it clicked in our mind that we had seen her before. She was plastered all over the street and broadcasted on every news channel in Britain. She was Sophie Barnwell - missing, presumed dead for the last two years! "Please help me," she murmured, as small tears rolled down her scarlet cheeks...

Isabel Reynolds (14)
Hodgson Academy, Poulton-Le-Fylde

The Dog

Part of me was missing. The lights dimmed, the spotlight shone... it was time to make miracles. I granted their wishes as I dazzled about. The show, the circus... I was a clown, a puppet on strings, I needed to escape. The old man laughed, "You cannot leave, it's dangerous out there but if you really want to see your familly then I will take you when sunlight comes!"
I hopped in his car and we drove away. We pulled up, there was my house. I walked through the gates and I became the dog I was...
"Ace, you're back!"

Archie Broadbent (12)
Hodgson Academy, Poulton-Le-Fylde

The Missing

"They'll never find me!" I reassured myself. But as I heard the footsteps gradually getting louder, I began to think otherwise. Beads of sweat were running down my face, my heart pounded against my chest and then there was a deafening silence... *Thud! Thud! Thud!* The knocking didn't stop. I frantically ran towards the window. Trying to hold the key as steady as I could in my hand, I threaded it through the lock. *Click!* As I forced myself through the window, I landed with a thud. That was the last thing I remember...

Sam Poulter (12)
Hodgson Academy, Poulton-Le-Fylde

Something Was Missing...

I recognised the voice talking; urging me to come into the house after months in hospital. Her eyes beamed at me in the nurturing, motherly way. Calm, steady eyes - like oceans encased in small, glass marbles. Her golden hair, braided in a loose plait, seemed to cruise on the midday breeze and a warm, colourful smile spread across her countenance. The emerald grass stood frozen in a glitter of frost, casting a peppering of splintered shadows across the front lawn like broken glass. But that was just a picture in my mind. Blindness: my new companion.

Phoebe Poulter (13)
Hodgson Academy, Poulton-Le-Fylde

Silence

Part of me was missing something; I was missing something that I could not live without... What would I do? Where would I go? I thought that the world was ending. The street was grey and the sky was black. The only source of light was the roaring fire in the distance. The only sounds were the faint cries of children looking for their families. Suddenly, the place fell silent. All I could hear was the flickering of the fire. I heard footsteps, getting closer and closer. Suddenly, something sharp scraped along my neck then there was total silence...

Rose Prentice-Bee (12)
Hodgson Academy, Poulton-Le-Fylde

The Hidden Truth

I had never presumed I was missing something. Disgusted at my untruthful parents, treated differently because I was unusual. I was also a pale-white skin colour. Always different from everyone. People wanted to know why I was strange, the truth was hidden deep inside my soul. Somewhere unknown. Strange, because I would lurk around spying on people I thought were unusual. My mind batted conflict. Part of me wanted to believe these distraught people and the other part of me didn't. I was lost. I couldn't take any more lies. I had no soul!

Josh Oxley (11)
Hodgson Academy, Poulton-Le-Fylde

The Missing

Missing, presumed dead... Jess (a girl in my year) disappeared last week and nobody knew what happened. Her parents contacted the police but they suggested she ran away. Everyone was doubtful. Our school planned a swimming trip (we go every year) in the local pond. It was all people were talking about. We all stripped down to our swimming costumes and hopped in. I felt something cold on my leg, it couldn't be! A snake? I screamed and scrambled to shore. My teacher called the police to come and remove it. It was a girl, it was Jess tied up!

Sam Rule (12)
Hodgson Academy, Poulton-Le-Fylde

Hotel Killer

The psychopathic laugh from the hotel owner digs into my nerves and turns into a horror scene. I was sceptical from the start, ever since the first stride into Hotel Appal. I thought that was a funny French word, I was wrong. You see, there were a lot of missing people in this area but my thick parents overlooked that and booked a hotel where the owner's a mass murderer. He's already drowned my parents! He is known as the 'Briny Killer' in this part of California because he drowns people in seawater and I am his next victim...

Archie Holroyd (12)
Hodgson Academy, Poulton-Le-Fylde

The Anniversary

It's been one year since it happened. My bones quivered as I dialled the number. "It wasn't my fault," I whimpered. The siren sounded, bright lights twinkled. People who I barely knew attempting to save my life. I was carried from my bashed and battered, crusty car to the crisp cleanliness of a yellow and blue van.

My eyes awakened when I first reached the place I needed to be at, as chaos and congestion struck the corridors. Within hours, I woke up. Half of my leg had vanished, my life would never be the same.

Lily-Rose Foy (12)
Hodgson Academy, Poulton-Le-Fylde

Missing

It was as if he was dead. His soul had been darkened to the point it was like there was no life left inside. Blankness. Behind his eyes was a wall of emotions. One by one, each brick fell apart. His body movements were unnatural as he walked up towards us. Pale white, his skin looked depressed. The look on his face was a horror. He continued to drag his heavy legs as he moved closer. I asked him, "Where's your English homework?"

A sudden alarm had hit his body as he began to twitch. He quietly said, "At home."

Josh Vickers (14)

Hodgson Academy, Poulton-Le-Fylde

Missing

Missing, presumed dead. I was out one night, the wind was forcefully pushing me and my belongings down the damp, freezing pavement when a middle-aged man approached me. His hair was black, slowly fading to grey. Illuminous. His eyes were glowing like a street lamp on a silent night. I would never forget those eyes. He was speaking to me, however, I wasn't listening because I knew what was happening. Why didn't I run away? I knew he was taking me somewhere and I knew I wouldn't be coming back. Goodbye Mum and Dad, I love you...

Grace Johnson (13)
Hodgson Academy, Poulton-Le-Fylde

Cliff-Hanger

They'll never find me... I'm on the edge of the Cliffs of Dover. Literally, I am dangling off the edge, hanging on for dear life. I'm a notorious criminal who has escaped from prison. The police are looking all over for me but I know that they will never find me. I hear footsteps above me like an elephant's. Panic starts to engulf me as the footsteps get nearer... A face creeps over the edge and panic takes over. My hands slip and all goes black before I recognise I am even falling... They'd found me and found me dead.

Fin Tupman (11)
Hodgson Academy, Poulton-Le-Fylde

Missing

'Missing, presumed dead.' Presumed dead, that's just false hope. As the headlines crackled onto the dust-engulfed screen, hysteria seeped into my mind. Oak frames are stained with the memories of the lost one and are now a reminder of the blistering pain. They now lie in a sea of the dead in the battlefields beating heart: the only place to find peace. But we are the ones who have suffered. Yes, they only have to mourn. Feelings of being whipped in two like a knife on soft flesh does not compare to it being your flesh...

Evie Panther (13)
Hodgson Academy, Poulton-Le-Fylde

Stuck

Why couldn't I remember? What happened? Where was I? Confused, I lifted up my hand to touch my face. There was blood trickling down my forehead. I tried to sit up, I couldn't. It was like my body was too heavy for me. What? As I looked around the dark room, there was nothing I could do. The first thing that came to my mind was to scream for help but no one answered. *Surely this can't be happening*, I thought to myself. This was all just a dream, right? It wasn't. But the thing was, I didn't know that...

Ellie Senior (12)
Hodgson Academy, Poulton-Le-Fylde

Disappear

The place was empty, or so I thought... Lightning struck at the chime of midnight, my head was pounding but set on one thing only. Trees were galloping, a tornado tearing leaves from trees like a child snatched from its parents. As I approached, the grave lit up with another great strike of lightning. Realisation trickled in through my eyes and into my brain. The impossible had happened. Before I knew it a cold, sharp point pressed against my pale cheek. I froze abruptly, the blade fell slowly. I saw a hooded figure. It was him...

Oliver Callaghan (14)
Hodgson Academy, Poulton-Le-Fylde

Missing

I told her not to meet him, I told her not to trust him, I told her everything! I called her, she never called back. I texted her, she never replied. I tried my best to find her, but never could. A week had passed without her around. Randomly I got a text... 'Unknown number' with the words: 'You're next'. I ran as fast as I could to get home. I stopped at a street light with a poster that had her face on. Above the picture were three words in big, bold, red writing it read: 'Missing, Presumed Dead'...

Lucy Pentelow (13)
Hodgson Academy, Poulton-Le-Fylde

Missing

Missing, presumed dead. Tears streamed down her face as she fell to the ground. The news she had received leaving a lump in her throat that dropped to the pit of her stomach. "Mum, I'm here! Why can't you see me?" It was no use, I just sat there glued to the ground, forced to watch her fall apart. It was like I was being punished, it was torture. Was I really gone? I gently kissed her on her forehead and told her I loved her one last time. Then she stopped crying and looked up...
"Elio...?"

Rosy Treasure (13)
Hodgson Academy, Poulton-Le-Fylde

The Unexpected Surgeon

Part of me was missing, my eyes weren't able to open and a mechanical-like buzzing was all I could hear. It was hot and I was walking through Madrid, then I smelt something. That was the last thing I could remember...
With all my power, I tried to open my eyes but I couldn't. Then freezing cold air ran through my right arm. Finally! Finally my eyes opened to three men in blue uniforms. Then I looked to my right, my arm was cut clean off. One of the men took their mask off. He looked too familiar... "Dad?"

Mischa Foster (12)
Hodgson Academy, Poulton-Le-Fylde

Lost

There I was, stranded on an empty island. I was considering how I got here, what I should do and how to escape if there was water surrounding the whole island! My threat was mainly dehydration. What could I drink? I felt dehydrated and drinking saltwater would make it worse. I decided to go into the forest and find some coconuts or bamboo. At this point, I was in excruciating pain. I felt sick and was about to faint. Then, suddenly, I found a tree full of coconuts. I grabbed a few of them. I smashed one and began drinking...

Reece Morley (13)
Hodgson Academy, Poulton-Le-Fylde

The Missing

I was running, the group behind me in hot pursuit. Three years ago every person of authority vanished, plunging the Earth into a dark abyss. I hadn't met this group before, one thing I knew though, they wanted me dead. I darted into Tesco and hid behind a counter. They walked in and started looking. Once they turned away I took my chance. *Bang, bang, bang, bang, bang.* I started panicking, I had killed five people. How could this have happened? There was only one option... I pointed the gun at my face and fired.

Harvey Wilson (12)
Hodgson Academy, Poulton-Le-Fylde

Abandoned In A Blink Of An Eye

The plane was empty, hollow. The light disappeared in front of me and then darkness surrounded me. Dust and dirt entered my lungs without an invitation. The Arctic air absorbed into my body, numbing my bones, blood and heart... frozen. The constant noise of drip, drip, drip and the clammer of rocks got crushed by the dramatic weight of what was above it. It felt like the colossal hole in the earth was closing in on me at a constant rate and eventually was going to crush me. Nobody knows where I am, nobody will ever find me.

Jayden James Gaskin (13)
Hodgson Academy, Poulton-Le-Fylde

I Can't Taste It!

I woke up. I went downstairs and made my toast. My toast was bland, I couldn't taste anything, not even my cranberry juice beside me. I thought nothing of it and carried on my day but it was getting more unusual. I started to get angry, very angry. I started to lash out at my teachers, my mind went blank. Why couldn't I remember? Suddenly I remembered part of me was missing. When I got home I received a letter from the doctor, it was tragic. It read: 'You have one year to live. Reason: missing sense/taste'.

Dillon Kelly (12)
Hodgson Academy, Poulton-Le-Fylde

Left

I couldn't believe I'd missed it. Like in a cave, all you could hear were my heavy breaths echoing off the cold stone walls of the immense station. Empty, lonely, quiet - I scanned the room which would usually be packed with people. All I did was go back to our grey car to collect the bag we had forgotten but once I had gotten back everyone was gone. The power had been shut down, the shutters covered the shops, there was no one in sight. Had my parents gone? My heart was beating against my chest. I had been left...

Isabelle Jacks (12)
Hodgson Academy, Poulton-Le-Fylde

Taken

The place was empty, I thought I was dead in minutes. Then he came in, a man with terror in his eyes. He came closer. Thoughts sprinted through my mind like bullets. What was he going to do? Who was he? Why had he taken me? A deep voice spoke, "There's no getting away now!" A feeling of both shock and fear shot through my spine. I was in an eerie basement with bland walls. Tension was building, each breath I took pain rose through my body. I cried but it was no use. I heard a voice. "It's over."

Joseph Hayes (12)
Hodgson Academy, Poulton-Le-Fylde

Lost

What happened? I thought. Slowly, I stood up and looked at my surroundings, trying to get an idea of what was going on. When my senses finally came back to me, I realised the excruciating pain I was in and it was at that moment I realised what was going on. *But where's everyone else?* I thought. *There must have been at least one hundred more people!* Suddenly a large pole of metal crashed right next to me and I heard the loud groaning of metal from above me. I looked up but it was too late...

Joe Edward Hardman (12)
Hodgson Academy, Poulton-Le-Fylde

What's That Sound?

They'll never find me, I'm not sure what to do, I'm lost. This place is deserted, no civilisation, no food or water, nor any contact but wait, what's that sound? Rustling, I think they have found me but no, it's some sort of animal. I guess I will have to eat it but wait, what's that sound? People, animals or wind? It's even more food. I can hear something in the sky. Are they looking for me? What are those blue and red lights? What is it in the sky? The police, they have found me, I am saved!

Alfie Burgess (11)
Hodgson Academy, Poulton-Le-Fylde

The Missing Piece

It was a Monday morning and I was having breakfast and doing a puzzle with my family. We were so close to finishing it but there was a piece missing. I trudged back upstairs to the study, which is where we kept the games and scoured the place... nothing. I stomped down the stairs more annoyed than when I came up and went into the living room. "I can't fi-" I said. But they weren't there. "Where are Mam and Dad?" I muttered. Suddenly I heard a noise, a noise that still haunts me to this day...

George Power (12)
Hodgson Academy, Poulton-Le-Fylde

Missing

They refused to let me go to the cinema. They left to go shopping; I was alone! I pulled out my phone and texted my friends I was coming. I tried on my very best dress, it was a little small, it would do.

I arrived. It was busy. Looking around, I glimpsed my friends and sat down. I remembered the long conversation.

Although, that was the last I remembered. My friends left to go get popcorn... Suddenly, a hand was over my mouth and my eyes shielded.

I woke up in an abandoned house with someone staring at me...

Millie Coates (11)
Hodgson Academy, Poulton-Le-Fylde

The Cookie Thief

I was fast asleep in my bed when I was woken by a loud bang coming from downstairs. I sat up in my bed, dripping with sweat I tiptoed to my bedroom door. As I opened my door I heard a voice coming from downstairs. "That looks nice, I'll take that." I quickly tiptoed back to my room and got into my closet to hide. I was sure I'd heard that voice before but I couldn't recall where from. Then I heard footsteps going into my brother's room so I ran into the room and saw my brother eating cookies!

Liam O'Rourke (11)
Hodgson Academy, Poulton-Le-Fylde

Soulless

It was like part of me was missing... I didn't know who I was and it was like I didn't have a soul without my family. They were gone and I was all alone. I was going to the College of Immortality, a place for supernaturals to help find themselves.

Two years later... I have been at the College of Immortality for two years now and I have made many friends. I have also learnt many things but a part of me is still missing and I don't know why... I start to leave. That voice... Mum? But she's gone...?

Olivia Crumblehulme (14)

Hodgson Academy, Poulton-Le-Fylde

The Lifeless Room

The place was empty. A blank canvas to begin working. However, there was no life. As if searching for an escape, I ran my hand down the creamy white wall. Lifeless. Sweeping my feet along the pearl-grey carpet, I stamped on it but it did not squirm. Lifeless. Flickering like an evil look in a murderous eye, the light seemed to know it could be killed by the flick of a switch. Pushing the cold button, I looked up to the light. Lifeless. Finally, I plunged the knife into the soft flesh of my nearest victim... lifeless.

Oliver Barrett (14)
Hodgson Academy, Poulton-Le-Fylde

Missing

I stared up at the Roberts statue towering above me. It was near the front of the museum so must be very important. It was made in honour of a girl that had gone missing on Tuesday, October 31st, 1977, and had never been found. Two teenage boys came running in with a slingshot and a dozen tomatoes. They were shooting them and the statue crumbled down. There was something inside it. Was it...? No! It couldn't be! It was the girl's dead body. How was she here? The girl jerked... How was she still alive?

Niamh Katie Roberts (11)
Hodgson Academy, Poulton-Le-Fylde

The Missing Piece

It was 1918 and the war had just passed. A miniature, frightened girl had come home after the pain of dreaded fighting. She always found a part of herself missing after the terrors of the last couple of years. One thing that would get her though was a singular photograph that she held so dearly.

Life moved on and so did the girl; she became a different person. However, there was one thing that she would do with no fault... She placed the picture down on the old, rusted gravestone. "I love you, Dad."

Emily Jane Davitt (12)
Hodgson Academy, Poulton-Le-Fylde

I've Got The Power

The place was empty, it was just me and my imagination. There was no way to get them back. A thought struck my mind... I'd wanted to be here for ages! I pinched myself... Nothing happened. I was insecure at the moment. Was there a way to get them back? Although I have dreamed about this moment forever, I'd realised how much I loved my family. I thought of them so much for about two days. After the two days, there was no need to imagine them. They were here. This is my imagination. I could do what I wanted.

Jack Burrill (12)
Hodgson Academy, Poulton-Le-Fylde

Gone, Forever

Part of me was missing; he was gone. It felt like someone had plunged a knife into my heart, shattering it again. Sitting there: alone. A pool of tears surrounding my body, unable to get him out of my head. There was no one to comfort me, to love or to spend the rest of muy life with. Everyone I ever loved was gone. My husband, taken by the war. I will always loathe the feeling of anyone going into that brutal place. Loving someone isn't just a feeling, it is a sensation that may well just drive you insane...

Mia Hanmore (12)
Hodgson Academy, Poulton-Le-Fylde

The Place Was Empty

The place was empty. The heirloom was missing. Panic struck me with a heavy blow, the piercing sound of the siren ran through my mind. There was no escape. Rattling shards of glass started dancing on the cold marble floor as the shouts of men flooded out of the chamber ahead. Desperately I searched for an escape that didn't end with my life in someone else's hands. Panic turned to nausea and I fell. A void of darkness consumed my vision and I was defeated by my final heist... I kept falling and falling...

Joseph Money (14)
Hodgson Academy, Poulton-Le-Fylde

They'll Never Find Me

What had happened? One minute I was walking back home then all of a sudden, five teenagers rushed me with baseball bats. I didn't even see them hit my head. I blacked out before I hit the floor. Now I'm pretty sure I'm in the back of a car, inside the boot. I told my family I'd see them today, what can I do? I can hear murmuring voices in front of me and I think they don't realise I'm listening. Then, shockingly, I hear my wife's voice. "Stop, let's dump the body here..."

Harry Neath (14)
Hodgson Academy, Poulton-Le-Fylde

I Knew It Was Mysterious

The place was empty, no lights, no cars, nothing but plain houses. To be fair, it was nine in the evening. No sound came from anything. The silence was deafening. The noise was scarce. I paced forward looking for lights. The round crescent of houses was terrifying like I'd walked into an entrance but no exit was to be found. Lights in the distance raced towards me. Two men in black jumped out, grabbed me and put me in the back of their van. I knew it was mysterious. I should have run but there was no way out.

Brandon Butterfield (11)
Hodgson Academy, Poulton-Le-Fylde

Criminal At Large

'Missing, presumed dead...' This is what the headline on the front page of the newspaper would say. Here I stand, on the edge of a cliff overlooking the sea, the fresh salty breeze on my face; this is what freedom feels like. Finally, after twenty long years in a cell with the highest security, I am free. They will never find me, they won't even try. Maybe I could live free forever. But someday I will return and take revenge. For now I am as free as a bird, ready to do as I please. I am a criminal...

Elsie Turner (11)
Hodgson Academy, Poulton-Le-Fylde

Missing

It was the summer of 2012, me and my friend were playing out in the garden. I remember asking if she wanted a drink, She said, "Yes, of course." I went and got the drinks, little did I know it would be the last time I'd speak to her. I came back and the place was empty. It was just me, both drinks still in my hand. Crying, screaming, hurting. I started to walk up the street but couldn't see anything. I searched everywhere. Called everyone I knew. Now it's 2017 and she's still missing.

Eva Tregonning (12)
Hodgson Academy, Poulton-Le-Fylde

Missing

The money was gone. It had vanished; it had disintegrated into thin air. Anxiety leaked through my veins. It suffocated my mind, sending a trickling sensation down my spine. He was after me, I knew it. Footsteps bounced off the walls, trying their utmost to escape the terror of the tunnel. Running, running faster than ever, as fast as my delicate legs could hold. Flooding in fear, my body became paralysed. It became impossible to escape this time. He stood right there in front of me. Not moving, nor smiling...

Nevaeh Bailey (11)
Hodgson Academy, Poulton-Le-Fylde

Missing

I calmly walked towards the door, praying they didn't see me or the trail of bodies in my wake. Once I crossed the threshold of my door, the sprint began.

I rushed towards the trees, the siren going off behind me, shouts ringing out while footsteps hit the ground. I took a leap of faith and landed in the forest but it wasn't over. Blood was shooting out from my calf but I had no option but to push on running. I saw a cliff in front of me and jumped into the icy waters below. I was now... missing!

Alfie Lee (14)
Hodgson Academy, Poulton-Le-Fylde

The Place Was Empty

The place was empty. No food. No water. No nothing. Just the air and space that filled the odourless void that was contained by the walls of the house. Rapidly I slammed the door behind me. With great urgency, I put a padlock on the door so I knew it was me and only me. In the silence, the violent thumping of my heart was the only sound. *Bang!* All light vanished. Ferociously a gust of wind threw me to the ground as if it had the force of a thousand elephants. I turned. The lock gone. The door open...

Noah Jebson (13)
Hodgson Academy, Poulton-Le-Fylde

The Missing

He'd been missing for months. One moment he was there, the next he was gone. It was the third week of trying to find my lost brother but it was no use. "Missing, presumed dead," they told me. But I couldn't think like that. I couldn't think that this search was all for nothing, that he was gone for good... This all happened previously and then, on Tuesday night, they found him. But I wasn't happy or relieved, I was scared, curious, unsettled. They had found his body, he was dead...

Niamh Morton
Hodgson Academy, Poulton-Le-Fylde

Missing Loafers

Part of me was missing, without those fluffy, fur-lined slippers. Luxury, comfort and warmth; they were so much more. It all began at the sleepover. We were getting ready for bed so I took my slippers off and I woke up to find my slippers gone. Who was the crime scene culprit? Was it a practical joke or was this a crime scene? We still could not find the slippers... Like Mr Tickles was underneath my foot, my foot started to tickle. I had forgotten I went for a drink in the night and put my slippers back on!

Zachary Shaw (12)
Hodgson Academy, Poulton-Le-Fylde

Discovered

They'll never find me. I'm hiding in a small, compact wardrobe in a hidden room. I am hidden, yet feel something off-putting but distant. I make out the noise of the faint taps that echo on the floor as footsteps and suddenly begin to panic... Shivers go down my entire spine. If I'm found I will be sent to that godforsaken place! No sign of escape lies upon my eyes, other than the open vent high, high up above me like a bird - out of reach. My heart drops as they open the door and discover me...

James Morris-Iliffe (12)
Hodgson Academy, Poulton-Le-Fylde

Listen

It's 7am and my alarm is going off like crazy. I rummage around my bedside table to press the top button. After that, it's time to trek to my wardrobe to throw on whatever I can feel for first. By now it's probably around 7:20am and I'm usually ready so I shout Mum to bring me my breakfast bar as I have never been able to find them myself. This takes me to 8:30am and that's the end, time to go to school. It's pretty ordinary as you can see but I can't, so I just listen!

Maddison Alice Caunce (13)
Hodgson Academy, Poulton-Le-Fylde

Gone

It was just a normal day. I woke up as normal, had breakfast and went to school. But something felt odd. Everyone was gone, it was so quiet.
I finally got to school, hoping that somebody would be there. But the place was empty, even the teachers weren't there. I knew that I was mean to everyone but I didn't think they'd all run away just because of me. I felt so guilty, I loved everyone that I ever met but didn't show it. Now I was the only one here and I didn't know what to do...

Olivia Wilde (12)
Hodgson Academy, Poulton-Le-Fylde

Eyes In The Dark...

They were here, I was the only one left. Alone, in this old, worn-out house. I'd been here for weeks, possibly even months. Ever since the lights went out. I was sat in the corner, my eyes hardly open. Their luminous, yellow eyes darting around me, destroying everything. They were approaching me, they got closer and closer... What could I do? I no longer felt alone. What were these things? Their eyes met mine and suddenly my emotions rushed away. They were all gone - missing. I was one of them now...

Lucy Montgomery
Hodgson Academy, Poulton-Le-Fylde

Where?

Part of me was missing, my brain. I thought nobody cared if I just disappeared, disappeared into thin air. Now I had a new life, three years on... I just remember my heart lurching out of my chest when I first vanished. I had had a funeral with no body. I was just the girl that disappeared. I now wanted to go home. Home to the subdued home of my parents', if they were still well. I carried the sadness on my shoulders everywhere I went. The deep darkness of my body overcame me. I decided to go home...

Grace Burgess (12)
Hodgson Academy, Poulton-Le-Fylde

The Missing

I slowly stood straight, my legs creaking like a door. I felt unable, powerless, climbing out of the damp pit I was in. I felt a tingle on my cheek, followed by a substance dripping to the ground. It was fresh blood. I spotted a large boulder in front of me, I could vaguely make out what was written on it. On the first line, it read: 'Forever missed'. What did that mean? Then there was a name: 'James Harding'. It was a grave and I recognised the name, it was mine. I had escaped my grave!

Katie Workman
Hodgson Academy, Poulton-Le-Fylde

It Was Over

I didn't care, I just needed to release my stress. I wanted to feel power. I didn't feel guilt, it felt right. I was standing in a puddle, a puddle of blood. It was the best feeling, people were scared of me. I felt invincible, powerful. My knife sliced through people like butter. Bodies were everywhere, I killed everyone who hurt me when I was younger, to show them how I felt. My heart dropped, I could hear sirens. I ran as fast as I could but it didn't matter because it was already over.

Alessio Ruocco (12)
Hodgson Academy, Poulton-Le-Fylde

Stranded

How did I get here? What happened? Why couldn't I remember? Maybe because I got hit so hard in the head. Dead. Missing. Alive. All that people thought, but I wasn't dead. I was alive but missing. I was kidnapped and left stranded in the middle of the ocean, with no food and no water at all except the disgusting salty water that made the ocean.

After the day in the horrible heat, I landed ashore. An old, wrinkly man peered over at me asking my name. I was thankful, he helped me get home.

Dylan William Nicholas (13)
Hodgson Academy, Poulton-Le-Fylde

Missing

They will never find me, I have been missing for days. They are crying for me to come back on camera but they were the ones to put me here, hiding me, isolating me from everyone else. Why? For money and fame! I'm down here struggling to breathe while they are up there saying they miss me! I must get out but they have blocked every single way out. I'm dehydrated and starving. They're slowly killing me and mentally abusing me, physically too! Hurting me at the age of seven. How could they?

Maddox Bellew (12)

Hodgson Academy, Poulton-Le-Fylde

The Mad Man

He was gone, the most dangerous man on the planet just disappeared! Sam Tyson, the man who killed twenty-four people in just one day, the mad man, was gone! There could only be one reason why. A bead of sweat ran down my forehead, I had survived the Coronavirus and now he needed me dead. Oh no! After I accidentally killed his brother, I was the only person he wanted and before he went to prison he let me know this and what he wanted to do to me. Sam Tyson was after me. I would be dead by sunrise...

Alfie Arden-Turner (12)
Hodgson Academy, Poulton-Le-Fylde

Hidden

They'll never find me hidden in plain sight. Lost. Like an isolated prisoner. Everything was going fine then I got angry and everything was gone. It's like I'm always on the run, from who? From me? I don't know what to do anymore. Where am I? Who am I? Life on the run from my old life, my perfect life, to find something better. But there is nothing better. But now it's gone, everything, and I am a murderer, a criminal. I am not me and I never will be. Is this what death is like?

Joseph Ball (11)
Hodgson Academy, Poulton-Le-Fylde

The Missing Memory

I woke to sirens, in a room I didn't know. Was I confused, scared, maybe dreaming? It took a while to fully wake. I wish I hadn't woken. Why was I here? What lay before me made me sick to the stomach. What happened? How did it happen? I was so scared I didn't think I was breathing for a minute. A bang on the door came. The police... No! I would get blamed, for all I knew I was framed! But how? I heard the door break, I didn't do anything though, but the weapon was in my hand...

Kayleigh Barnes
Hodgson Academy, Poulton-Le-Fylde

The Missing

I was playing hide-and-seek when it happened. I sprinted to a room and I discovered something. The room was bare. I revealed an old, rustic wardrobe and I clambered into it. *They'll never find me,* I thought; well I guessed that was true! I got sucked into another dimension! It was a world with chocolate rivers and edible trees and grass. The sky was pink and people were half-human and half-animal. Why couldn't I remember what happened? A part of me was missing... my family!

Madison Evans (11)
Hodgson Academy, Poulton-Le-Fylde

The Missing

Shivering in the dark, the screams and tears never left me...
It was a summer's day, I had lived with my mum since I was
born. Apparently my father never wanted me so he ended
up just leaving us. I had been to a party last night but it did
not go to plan.
Suddenly, reality hit me. How was I going to escape? How
did I even get here? I heard it... He whispered a name to me,
my name? Whoever it was wanted to see me. Slowly he
removed his mask. Then I realised who it was... Dad?

Abbie Williamson (11)
Hodgson Academy, Poulton-Le-Fylde

Senseless

Why couldn't I remember? I don't know why it happened. Now all I seem to remember is that it was a normal day until... it went black. It changed everything and I know I won't be able to get it back. Some people don't actually realise how lucky they are. Well, compared to me anyway. My family tried to assist me along the way but it didn't help. One day, I arrived home but nobody was there. I thought they got fed up with me. I was right. I am alone now! But also blind...

Tom Healey (11)
Hodgson Academy, Poulton-Le-Fylde

The Story

A part of me was missing, I was dizzy, sick, in a terrifying state. It seemed to be a bunker but I had total amnesia and couldn't feel my tongue. My leg was chained to the floor, the padlock that was keeping me was about to collapse so I smashed it open. *Boom!* I ran out of the house, breaking the door down, my body felt like collapsing... I had been drugged. I looked up into the window, staring at a familiar face. Who was it? My eyes flashed, covering me in eternal darkness.

Harry Butcher (14)
Hodgson Academy, Poulton-Le-Fylde

Only Myself To Blame

The place was empty. The clock spinning rapidly. Creatures appearing, disappearing. Where was I? Figures lured me towards the darkness. A tap on the shoulder was all it took to drive me insane. I turned around, I felt the creature taking over. He told me to kill, to attack. I was free for a moment. I looked down, lying there dead was... me! It took me a moment to realise I was the creature. I fell to my knees, crying for help. I was gone, lost. The link was missing. I was dead and gone.

Skye Philburn (12)
Hodgson Academy, Poulton-Le-Fylde

Debt

I search my house and ransack my drawer. I don't get it, it's supposed to be here! Panic fills my body like a fountain. What am I going to do? They know exactly where I live, where I go to school and where my family are. Why did I ever agree to this? I take my bag out of my wardrobe and frantically throw clothes into it. I have to get out of here now. My parents will kill me if they know what I've done. Rapidly I run down the stairs for the last time - the money is gone!

Imogen Lyne (15)
Hodgson Academy, Poulton-Le-Fylde

Missing

My whiskers twitch at all the sights and sounds in the city as I cower here in a dark place. The little humans who come near are the worst... except for my little humans. Slowly I curl up, the cold ripping my strength away from me. In my sleep, I play back the times when we'd go to the big white ball in the sky. I purr like a lion. I can't wait to see them but then... I do! They're here! They're here to take me to the big white ball once again so... we fly.

Isabella Hill

Hodgson Academy, Poulton-Le-Fylde

Dream

Why couldn't I remember? Once a paramount utopia has now dissipated into a hideous monstrosity! Our government has corrupted into disaster. I have run away, I thought I needed to. I am running for my life...

When I arrive I shake at what I see. I am mortified. Is it... is it? It is! Once a cute dog but now it's all bloody and dead. All its organs lying on the floor from before.

Why couldn't I remember? It was all a dream but now it had turned real...

Arron North (14)
Hodgson Academy, Poulton-Le-Fylde

I Can't Hear You!

I remember a once chaotic world, a world that was full of sounds, lovely and horrible. I remember the words my dad used to tell me, "Never take anything for granted." I'll never be able to hear those great words again. I remember the beautiful words the birds used to sing and the screams of people, but all of that has gone. A part of me is gone. Music, which was my life and career, is now gone, the sound has gone. If only I hadn't made that mistake...

Ben Hoyle (13)
Hodgson Academy, Poulton-Le-Fylde

Money

The money was gone... As I walked to find a clue I saw that there was a footprint and I knew straight away that I may find the money as I carried on walking. I saw that a car was outside, I looked inside the door and the man's wallet had everything inside. The man's name was Dave. Suddenly, I heard a bang, I grabbed my gun and walked towards the sound, then a man ran with a bag full of money! I shot him and grabbed the money and ran! What would happen to me...?

Amelia Ashworth (12)
Hodgson Academy, Poulton-Le-Fylde

Drowned

Part of me was missing, I didn't know what to do when the police had told me they had found a body. My heart dropped. I, for a minute, thought it was her. Our life together flashed before my eyes. What if it was her? Like washing out of a dryer they pulled her body out of the pond. What if she took my words too seriously... what if this was all my fault? Blood, skin, bones: my sister was so much more than that. She was my best friend who I let go...

Amelia Palmer (12)
Hodgson Academy, Poulton-Le-Fylde

The Return

The silent screams were deafening. Everyone seemed to have something to say but the room remained in an inimitable awkwardness. They didn't know where I was; it was going to stay that way. The quiet vibration of an officer's phone sparked a casual chit-chat amongst them. I was so close to them, yet the furthest away I had ever been. Their streaming tears only motivated my cantankerous plan they would soon star in. They'd never find me...

Charlotte Gittins (15)
Hodgson Academy, Poulton-Le-Fylde

Midnight

The sun shone brighter than ever before. Children playing with their friends, refusing to come inside. Teenagers euphoric and making memories that would last forever. Everyone wishing for summer to come. But I'm the opposite, I wish I could have known it would all come to an end. I'm trapped in my house, hiding away from the sun. The only time I can leave is at night. At night when the stars shine and the sun is nowhere to be seen...

Lauren House (13)
Hodgson Academy, Poulton-Le-Fylde

Why?

Midnight had struck, searchlights were everywhere, sirens were deafening my ears, she was gone. Memories flickered back through my head from last night, the blood dripped down her neck, the pain she was going through and the look on her face, what had I done? The knife sliced through her body and crushed through her bones. Why did I do this to the innocent girl? I tried to escape from this nightmare but it was too late. I miss my sister...

Jessica Ramsden (12)
Hodgson Academy, Poulton-Le-Fylde

The Missing

Why can't I remember why I frighten babies or why I am known as the 'Beast of Humanity'? All I can remember is getting hit by a car and now this. Half of the world is gone from just one move! My head is sizzling as if I know the cause but not actually remembering. All I know is that I'm considered a baby killer or a human Hoover! My head is starting to sizzle again but differently this time. I know who did it... me!

Lucas Wilmot (11)
Hodgson Academy, Poulton-Le-Fylde

A Way Out?

They'll never find me. This place is horror-struck. Who is this revolting stranger and why is he in this must shadowy room with me? Why am I so tightly tied up? I squirm frantically without making much noise. This rope is grasping too tightly onto me.

Ring, ring, ring... No, this can't be happening. He has awoken. It is essential for me to escape. Although I have an extremely little amount of time to do so...

Katerin Hiffe (12)
Hodgson Academy, Poulton-Le-Fylde

The Money Was Gone...

The money was gone... I thought to myself, *how?* The police were stood with my parents talking about what happened. Then suddenly I saw my dad, who I trusted all my life had just taken a gun from the police and had run away from all of us. I tried to chase my dad and ask him why but he was already gone. My mum sat down with me and told me the shocking truth about my dad. I ran upstairs and hid. My dad was a robber.

Archie Walsh (11)
Hodgson Academy, Poulton-Le-Fylde

The Journal

As I walked to the door I reached over to the table of which my mother's picture lay to tell her about my day, but it was not there! It was missing! I gazed around the empty room... Out of the corner of my eye, I saw a shimmer in the rubbish and my dad's journal. I wondered why it was there. I decided to read through it and what I found was horrifying, I felt my heart sink to my stomach. How could he do that...?

Lauren Murray (12)
Hodgson Academy, Poulton-Le-Fylde

The Missing Village

The place was empty. The only thing you could see was the bare white walls. Moving quickly, they headed down a narrow hall. A lot had changed since they entered the lone house. Blood had covered the floors, but that wasn't the most daunting thing. What surprised them the most was the first room. Every single person who went missing in the missing village was there, not alive, but dead...

Mary-Anne O'toole (12)
Hodgson Academy, Poulton-Le-Fylde

Missing, Presumed Dead

Missing, presumed dead... All of this started just three months ago, my father got sent to prison. My family and I were devastated. Then suddenly, this morning, we received a call from the prison. My father became a prisoner and broke free. They said he'd been gone for over a week and still had not been found. I had never been more scared in my life. Where was he? Was he alive...?

Ella Chalk-Derby (12)
Hodgson Academy, Poulton-Le-Fylde

Flight

The plane was empty, not a living soul apart from my own. I thought I was on a flight to California but it turned out there was a terrorist on board. I was lucky to be alive but I wouldn't be for much longer. With the thoughts of my parents not being able to find me hurt. They wouldn't last a day without me being alive. They wouldn't be able to find me... no one would...

Cohen Ballentine (12)
Hodgson Academy, Poulton-Le-Fylde

Covid-19

The place was all empty, it was cold and dark. Then I saw it in the distance... *Home Bargains* - The sign was so bright, I could see it from afar. I went over to the bright sign and thought about grabbing some hand sanitiser to kill 99.9% of the bacteria on my hands. I went in and saw one bottle of hand sanitiser. I ran over and slipped in front of everyone. The hand sanitiser went everywhere and everyone started to fight in the middle of the shop over the hand sanitiser. My hands were still bacteria-infested!

John Dutch (16)
Montrose Academy, Montrose

Gym

Gym's fun, in my opinion. To do it you need a gym kit. Gym kits can vary, I wear a T-shirt and shorts, they're in a blue bag. One day, my kit got stolen. My parents were worried because apparently my T-shirt was 'as expensive as anything'. My mum told me to go and find it but I did not know where to look. I went to the lost and found. Nothing. I went to the sports centre. Nothing. I went home disappointed. As I walked into my house my mum said, "Guess what? I found it in your bedroom!"

Roan Angus (13)
Montrose Academy, Montrose

All Over The World

My teddy bear is gone. Mum says he is wandering the streets of Paris and is trying snails (yuck!). Dad says he is helping NASA build a rocket so we can go to space and meet aliens. Granny says he is travelling the world to collect her more stamps. Sister says he is in my room because it is too messy and Brother says he's been stolen and is being fed to sharks! I don't know where he went. I will find my teddy bear even if I have to look all over the world!

Paige Buchan (17)
Montrose Academy, Montrose

Ringletted

Missing posters swarmed the streets. On every tree, on every lamp post. The water-damaged image of a ringletted, curled dog gazed up through glassy eyes through the forever thinning paper. Locked behind the page, the strict voices of news reporters crackled through the TV screen before looming in front of my eyes. Guilt should have washed over me, but it didn't. Fear should have flooded over me, but it didn't. Not even sadness shattered over me when the little girl with thick plaits had tears streaming down her cheeks. The ringletted, glassy-eyed dog shuffled on my lap. No.

Hannah Cameron (13)
Olchfa Comprehensive School, Sketty

Isolated

Hands shaking, heart pounding, she delved into her pockets frantically searching every corner, soon realising that her worry stone was gone. Anxiously she clenched her fists as tears streamed down her pale cheeks. Dark, grey clouds started to surround her as the rain came crashing down. She trembled to the ground, feeling isolated and alone. She rehearsed breathing techniques but the tears only became rivers. She gasped desperately at the ever-thinning air. Her mind began to spiral, her palms were sweaty and she shook until the lights went out.

Heidi Rodenburg (12)
Olchfa Comprehensive School, Sketty

Missing

In a creepy supermarket just down the road, the potatoes are missing! Carrot and Banana have to hunt down their missing friends...

Carrot and Banana are going to aisle four, the last place they were seen. One thing that Carrot notices is that the bag they were in was cut open and policeman scissors are now on the case.

As they are walking away, Carrot notices a dirt trail and they go to aisle 7.

"There they are!" shouts Carrot and just in time because the supermarket opens in two minutes. But who did this? Do you know?

Jadyn Coates (12)
Parkhall Integrated College, Antrim

Wiped

It all started normally, then a flash of black came upon us. It was like this for years. Everyone was safe, apart from Bella. Search parties went out looking and a dead body was found and identified as her. Three days passed and she was buried but everyone's memory of her was gone. All of a sudden, a girl called Ember appeared out of nowhere and knew a lot about her, this was very suspicious but soon things settled back to normal after a while. No one knew what was coming next or what caused all of this to happen...

Saffron Woods (12)
Parkhall Integrated College, Antrim

The Town Myth

It had been three years since Sophia Grimer had gone missing. I must confess, I do think of the number of people who have gone missing in this town, such as Micky Roland. There has always been a myth in our town, the legend goes that there was once a hiker that was trapped up there, never to come down. Now he eats wildlife and humans we are told. Come to think of it, it is mainly children that go missing, rather than adults. But this summer, I want to find out. It is my responsibility, it's my only destiny...

Jack Daley-Beck (14)
Parkhall Integrated College, Antrim

John Goes Missing

We heard the sirens go off, I was terrified. All we did was burn down Farmer Joe's fence. I heard the sirens getting extremely close. John and I put on our darkest outfits, hoping the police wouldn't realise it was us. We were hiding in the forest, beside the farm. John screamed at me to run but I got trapped on a branch and couldn't get out. John ran ahead without me and I got caught and was taken to court the next day. I never found out where John went. I hope John is still alive today...

Ryan Empey (13)
Parkhall Integrated College, Antrim

My Way Home

They'll never find me, a man came last night and I can't quite remember what happened. All I remember is that I was walking home from school, I'm now in an empty room and I'm tied down by my arms to the bed. There is a doctor standing right beside me, I don't know what to do. My heart is pounding and my feet are freezing. I just want to go home to my mum and eat her nice warm chicken curry. I beg the doctor to take me home. They move me, I think I'm going home. Help.

Eva Hamitlon (13)
Parkhall Integrated College, Antrim

Lost

I was staring at the empty school in astonishment, I was so confused, I turned round to go home. When I got there, my mum wasn't there, no one was. They were all gone. About two hours later of looking for someone, anyone, I finally admitted to myself that I was the only one left. I didn't know what I was doing or why I was left, all I knew was that I needed to figure this one out on my own. It wasn't going to be easy but the whole world depended on me...

Sophia Dundee

Parkhall Integrated College, Antrim

Silence

The howling wind blew while the dark moon shone in the east. Me and Keira were frightened, dead still. Keira wouldn't go to sleep so we went to guard. Keira wouldn't go to sleep so I did. The fire was going out slowly, the tents were not so strong so they were going down slowly. Keira said, "I think we camped in the wrong area."
I said, "This place does look dodgy!"
It was not long till morning but then we heard a stick crack.
I said, "I think someone's there, aim the gun and shoot..."
There was no response...

Olivia Heath (12)
St John Baptist CIW High School, Aberdare

I'm Sorry, Darling

I froze. My heart's speed began to increase. I frantically looked around, I heard something, I know I did. Or was it just me being paranoid? It must just be me being worried. If it was the police they would have gotten me already. I still didn't want to stick around, even if it wasn't the police. I forced my legs to move. Still shaken from what I thought I heard I pulled out the last of my water. I told myself I would save it but I couldn't help it. My tongue was dry, like sandpaper. "I'm sorry, darling..."

Madeleine Mold (14)
St John Baptist CIW High School, Aberdare

Missing

I couldn't believe I couldn't find her, she could be anywhere! I couldn't stop thinking about it. I had to try, I had too! The next day, I was watching the news when I heard her name. She had been missing for two days. I wondered where she was. Next, I went to my friend's house to see if she had seen her. Bad news once again. No one had seen her!

That night I couldn't sleep. I turned on the news to see if there were any further updates. I couldn't believe what I heard... she was dead!

Amy Smith (11)
St John Baptist CIW High School, Aberdare

The Red House

Everything around me was pitch-black. I was alone and terrified. This was the only way to get home from the park and unfortunately, none of my friends lived by me. Still walking through the darkness I heard something behind the tree. I reached for my phone in my pocket to turn on a flashlight but it was dead. I hesitantly walked over to the tree and saw a woman. Her eyes were blood-red. I saw she was holding a knife and I screamed in terror.

I opened my eyes, all I saw was red, this place was covered red...

Bailey Smith (12)
St John Baptist CIW High School, Aberdare

Missing Dog

The wind was howling, the storm was loud, frightening all the people in the house, running around like mad.
One family were in their home, playing games when the big, loud storm came. They all got scared so the dog ran away. The family didn't notice and they went to bed. The next morning, the little girl went to feed the dog and she noticed the dog was gone. She ran upstairs to tell her dad and mum that their dog was missing. They looked at the cameras to look for Charlie but they never found him.

Keira Taylor (12)
St John Baptist CIW High School, Aberdare

The Bear

One morning, I was getting ready for a festival, it was a rock one. About twenty minutes later, I was there. My friend went to the toilet. At 2:30 I went to get a drink, I came back from getting a drink. I was enjoying the music so much I got carried away. It was 4 o'clock, I couldn't find my friend so went to the toilet and said, "Has anyone seen my friend?" Then a big bear came down the hill and I followed it. Its footprints led me to a dead body with his head gone...

Jack Salmon (12)
St John Baptist CIW High School, Aberdare

I Got Kidnapped

This place was empty, where was I? Where were my friends? I couldn't find my phone, I shouted for help but no response. I was scared. I heard a bang. Who was it? All I saw was a tall shadow and then I heard police sirens. Were they looking for me? I shouted help but nobody came to help. I tried to move around then I found a lock and a flashlight. I turned it on and tried loads of lock combinations and one worked. I got out and I tried to find my way home. Finally, I was home.

Ruby Jones (12)
St John Baptist CIW High School, Aberdare

Gone

It was 12:44 at night, I was asleep until my alarm went off. It was funny because my alarm clock was set for 7am. I thought it was my sister! Then suddenly, a song went off. It was a little bit croaky and I didn't recognise it. Then I saw a black figure, I thought it was my sister so I said, "Go away, get back to your room!" Then the masked figure came closer, I said, "Go away!" once again but I noticed the figure had a knife. He grabbed me and I was gone.

William Thomas (12)
St John Baptist CIW High School, Aberdare

Kidnapped

It was a cold Saturday morning and the birds were chirping. I went into my son's bedroom, he wasn't there so I ran downstairs and told my wife and we started searching the house. No sign of him. I went to look out into the woods. I went to get my torch and then I heard a scream coming from deep in the woods. Was I ever going to find him? I kept on hearing strange voices as I got deeper and deeper into the woods. There was no sign of him. Was he dead...?

Isabella Towers (12)
St John Baptist CIW High School, Aberdare

Kidnapped

It was 3am, I woke up suddenly from a crash. At first I ignored it then the same thing happened. I was starting to get scared and nervous. There was a loud knock on my door and I hid under my bed cover. I heard the door open but was too scared to move. Then a man took the bed cover, put his hand over my mouth and took me away. I was in his car going really fast and... *bang!* We had crashed. I managed to get out of the car and ran home. I made it home.

Ciaran Chiggey (11)
St John Baptist CIW High School, Aberdare

Gone Forever!

They will never find me, I am gone forever. I have heard the police are looking for me and I heard my family are worried. I have been gone for about a week now. I have been hiding in a cave near the road. Oh no, is that what I think I can hear? Police sirens! I better run or they'll find me. I see a car, I'm going to get into the car. Now they are coming up. I'm in the car and I drive away. I am still missing, I knew this would happen...

Theo Christopher (12)
St John Baptist CIW High School, Aberdare

No Chance

Her eyes flew open, but she couldn't see anything. She tried to move her hands but they were painfully tied up. Panic rose inside her, spreading from her chest to her fingers, drowning her in despair. She didn't know what to do. "Why can't I remember?" she said. Nothing made sense. She couldn't remember a thing. She felt a blindfold wrapped around her head. Then she heard laughter. She desperately moved around, trying to get free. She knew deep inside her she wouldn't escape. She tried to scream but it was pointless. She knew she wouldn't see daylight again.

Pia Aylas Burghard (12)
St John's Academy, Perth

Nothing...

The place was empty... I felt something was missing. When searching the house, it started to fade away. I was terrified, fear filled my body. My body was stiff.

Ten minutes later, the house was almost gone. Melting like ice in winter. My hands were starting to disappear. I realised this was it for me. I sat by myself and waited, waited and waited. Silence, until it was the end of me. The last couple of seconds until I too faded. I started to breathe heavily, sinking down. Finally, I took my last, short breath into the arms of death...

Rholmark Colanse (12)
St John's Academy, Perth

The Place Was Empty

The place was deserted. The streets were deserted. There was no sound of kids playing there. There were no people anywhere. The shops were closed, the lights were off and the doors were shut. There were no aeroplanes in the sky, there were no birds, the town was totally silent. I could see no buses at all, this town was totally empty. I was really scared, where was the local market? There were no stalls. Where was the old lady selling eggs and the young man selling soup? There were no plants, it was very dull. I must go home.

Olivia McNaughton (12)
St John's Academy, Perth

Found

The place was empty so I stayed there. I heard a knock at the door and a low rusty voice started to speak. "I know you're in there!" I kept quiet and held my breath, I did not move, I froze. Next thing I know, a man came bursting through the door. I stayed still, I hid. He left. As soon as I moved the man ran back in searching, looking for the box. Luckily he didn't notice me, he was desperate. He threw over the chairs, emptied the drawers onto the floor. I hid and held my breath...

Marcus John MacNeill (12)
St John's Academy, Perth

Missing 23.4

The ransom note arrived It was stained with blood. It said: 'Missing but not gone'. But who? Suddenly I remembered, I phoned my only friend. She did not answer... Oh god, I better go check on her. I calmly went to her house but it seemed more scary, more creepy, more lonely. I knocked at the door, when I heard a scream from the other side of the street... I was so scared, I did not have the guts to go and look. I ran, it felt like running for miles. I felt like never stopping. Never...

Hanna Długołęcka (13)
St John's Academy, Perth

The Promise

Once there was a cat named Skippy. She was five years old and was not a normal cat, she was a magical cat that could fly. She accidentally turned the TV on and some news came on about a golden ring being stolen and the detective who was a frog needed help to try and get it back. Skippy got a letter and it was to get help from Detective Frog. She made a potion of teleportation so they went to the place and fought the bad guys and the world was saved. She was then helpful to Earth forever.

Olivia Elder (13)
St John's Academy, Perth

My Uncle House

The money was gone, I was sure that I left it at my uncle's, under his bed. It couldn't be gone. There was a piece of paper under the bed, I was confused, there was a part missing on the corner of the paper. It said to find the other piece? My uncle's house was so big I could not even find it! My uncle was gone, he was at his house a few days ago and I think that he stole the money and ripped the corner of the paper for me to find. But why me?

Georgie Balla (12)
St John's Academy, Perth

Location Unknown

Missing, the government had taken away emotions. Stolen them! A sense of soul stripped from everyone. Each individual left empty, lost in thought. Why? Happiness. The higher-ups ruled unfairly. They said we should earn emotion through age. "As soon as you turn 18," they explained, "you can have them back." It was a mass murder. Everyone over 18 assassinated. The emotions? The bodies? All hidden in the same place; missing. Young people trapped in their minds, trying to remember life before it all turned horrible. Memories started to fade away. Emotions, bodies, memories? All in the same location.

Chloe Smith (12)
St Richard's Catholic College, Bexhill-On-Sea

Person Unknown: Missing

They'll never find me. Nothing, nobody can. If they do, they will be gone. Missing. Abducted. I will take them to a place so beautiful they won't want to leave. Then they will be gone for good. No one comes out alive. He will tear them to pieces, letting them no longer be a prisoner in our world. Then they will be remembered as the person gone missing. Heaven forbid if the body is discovered. They will see the torn-up carcass of someone found. Unlike me. No longer hiding, no longer missing. But they won't find me, no way.

Nico Luscombe (12)
St Richard's Catholic College, Bexhill-On-Sea

Gone

I was the only person left, the world had come to a standstill. Everyone vanished! The virus had taken everyone hostage and it was never going to give them back. My family, friends, the whole world - all gone! We had all been on lockdown, except people like my mum. She had to go outside into the brutal world. How I begged her not to but duty called. One day, she came in coughing. The next, my brother. Soon they were dead. I stayed at home, locked from the outside universe. Two months later, I went out. Everyone was gone!

Jeseena Joseph (13)
St Richard's Catholic College, Bexhill-On-Sea

Missing Soul

I am missing, I've been presumed dead. Am I a ghost? Over time people have forgotten about my existence. I chose to run away, I stay off the radar. They will never find me. I don't want to go back, back there, that place was like a living hell. They abduct you and force you to work. If you disagree, well, that's too bad for you because you don't want to. I want to find my parents, but yet I have a sense that they are out there or they might have turned into monsters like the rest of humanity!

Oliver Ardley (12)
St Richard's Catholic College, Bexhill-On-Sea

Ghost Town

I sit on a train, I look out of the window to see a lit-up city, but then one light stands out brighter than the others. It is red lightning. It destroys the Earth and turns people into monsters. My train falls and I land in a military base. Most humans have gone missing. I am not scared, I'm just full of hatred. I search and find some power armour and a pump-action shotgun. I am ready for war. The monsters break in and I pump my shotgun and brutally kill them all. I'm now ready for more...

Alex Hards (13)
St Richard's Catholic College, Bexhill-On-Sea

And Then She Was Gone

"You cannot tell anyone, Violet."

"Why, Rose? I thought you were happy at home?" I sobbed, trembling in the hammering rain behind the yellow taxi.

"Well, I'm not! My parents hate me. I'm always insulted by my siblings, I don't feel a part of the family!" Rose wailed, slamming the car door, driving out of sight. Gone.

It had been a month, panic flowed through the town. "Where is she?" they asked. Tugging in my stomach was guilt, never leaving me.

A year passed. Missing, presumed dead? My best friend long gone, my heart sinking and aching almost every day.

Phoebe Hands

Thomas Telford School, Telford

I Found It At The Bottom Of The Lake

My mind was churning as I meandered down the woodland path in total mental dismay. How could it happen? Someone must have found it. Someone knew. The diary missing - the secret out! The thief must have known where it was. They must have watched me. With that, paranoia began to manifest. Alarmed, I pounded through the undergrowth. I was in danger. Cheeks flushed by the fierce wind, I arrived at the oak. Hurling my hand inside, I desperately felt around. My breath latched... until I skimmed it. Brandishing the locket, I vowed to keep the spirit with me, forever prisoner.

Lily Dodds (12)
Thomas Telford School, Telford

The Dark Room

"Where am I?" The place is empty, I'm alone, I think. Writing. Red writing is on the wall behind me. As my cold, frosty body swivels around I notice what it says: 'I'm inside your space, I know everything!' I quickly turn back around as a noise is made in the other dark corner. I see it, the faceless body. Too afraid to carry on staring, I turn back around to notice the words have changed. Now all it says is: 'Missing' in big, bold letters. Nobody knows what I have done. They are in the room with me...

Freya Preece (12)
Thomas Telford School, Telford

Mistreated

Sometimes I wished I was dead. My grandparents were the only ones who took me for who I am. Every night, I cried myself to sleep. I got nothing from my mother or father and I just wanted it all to end. I needed to find happiness. Somewhere, there would be someone like me, alone. Someone else who dreaded the day ahead. I had a plan, a plan to run away. Somewhere they wouldn't ever find me. Hmmm... yes! My grandparents' graves. I headed for the forest, my face hit the ground. I saw nothing but darkness. Where was I?

Milly April Slater (13)
Thomas Telford School, Telford

YOUNG WRITERS INFORMATION

We hope you have enjoyed reading this book – and that you will continue to in the coming years.

If you're a young writer who enjoys reading and creative writing, or the parent of an enthusiastic poet or story writer, do visit our website **www.youngwriters.co.uk**. Here you will find free competitions, workshops and games, as well as recommended reads, a poetry glossary and our blog. There's lots to keep budding writers motivated to write!

If you would like to order further copies of this book, or any of our other titles, then please give us a call or order via your online account.

Young Writers
Remus House
Coltsfoot Drive
Peterborough
PE2 9BF
(01733) 890066
info@youngwriters.co.uk